PERFECT CATCH

N.R. WALKER

BLURB

Calvin Lynch and Troy Hoffman have been best mates since they were fourteen years old. They're both hard-working tradesmen, both love weekends away fishing, both gay, but have never been single at the same time. Until now.

What is supposed to be a weekend away fishing with a group of mates, changes at the last minute when friends bail out in an attempt to give Cal and Troy some alone time.

With more than just hooks on the line, can these two see what's been right in front of them the whole time?

The Perfect Catch is a short story about falling for your best friend hook, line, and sinker.

COPYRIGHT

DEDICATION

To the wonderful folk in the M/M Daily Grind.
This story wouldn't exist without you.

AUTHOR NOTE

This was previously released as part of the *It Was Always You* anthology, released 2016.
It is now released as a single title. No additional content has been added.

PERFECT
CATCH
N.R. Walker

———— •ı• ————

CHAPTER ONE

"HEY, can you grab the other end of this?" Troy asked. He climbed on his knees under the canopy into the back of his four-wheel-drive utility. He gripped one end of the long folded tent that leaned against the tailgate and waited for me to help with the other.

"Sure." I lifted the bottom end, and together we slid the tent onto the tray of his ute. I helped him load everything else on, getting ready for our weekend of camping out and fishing in the mountains.

I'd just called by his place to drop off the food for our trip and to see if he needed any last minute things. It was Thursday evening, and we were leaving at sunup the next day. "You sure you don't need me to get anything else?" I asked.

He pointed his chin toward a carton of Tooheys Extra Dry on the floor of his garage. "Just those."

I picked up the box of beer and slid it on the tray toward him. "Need ice for the beer?"

"Nah, we'll grab it from a servo on the way, yeah?"

I nodded. "What about your fishing rods?" His fishing rod holder was a two-metre length of PVC pipe, eight inches in diameter. The fishing rods simply slid into it, a screw cap at each end making them secure and well protected.

"I'll fix that up on top," he replied, sliding out of the back of his ute. Using the back tyre of the ute as a step, he grabbed the top rail of the canopy and effortlessly lifted himself up. "Pass it up for me?"

I held the long pipe along the roof of the canopy steady, and Troy fixed it with ratchet clamps. We'd done this so many times, gotten ready to go camping, that we barely needed words. We just kinda knew what the other was thinking. I'd known Troy Hoffman since the eighth grade, been mates since then too. We grew up and still lived in this country town. Life hadn't always put us on the same page in the ten years I'd known him, but we somehow always ended up hangin' out.

He'd been the only other gay kid I'd known when I was fourteen. He caught me checking out the school's polocrosse captain, and when I thought he was gonna punch me, he just swallowed hard and said, "He's hot, isn't he?" And we were inseparable after that. We were never together in the boyfriends-sense. We kept each other's secret until we were both ready to come out. He only had his mum to tell, and she took it like she was relieved he'd finally told her. My folks were okay with it; well, my mum and sister were fine with it. I think my dad was just relieved I was still a *man's man*. I was still keen to do my building apprenticeship and was one of the hardest hitting guys on our rugby team. I think my old man thought all gay men had a swish to their hips. But when he realised it didn't change a single thing about me, he said he was fine with it. I had to wonder if he'd still accept me if I was more flamboyant. I'd never really thought parents' love should have limits, but apparently my dad's might have.

Troy jumped down and clapped his hand on my shoulder. "You okay?"

I scrubbed my hand over my face, trying to clear my head. "Yeah."

"You need this weekend," he said, opening the passenger door. "It'll take your mind off... you know."

Off what? "Oh." I scoffed out a laugh. "No, it's not that. I wasn't even thinking about that."

Troy eyed me cautiously, but then proceeded to lean into his truck and rifle through the centre console, giving me a great view of his arse and thighs. He was wearing an old T-shirt and some footy shorts and his usual work boots. He was a mechanic by trade. He kept fit by running and playing soccer on weekends. His body was trim and tanned, muscular in all the right places. He'd always been the good-looking kid at school. He still was. With short brown hair, eyes the colour of burnt honey, and a killer smile that pressed a dimple into his left cheek.

Everyone always assumed we were a couple. Where there was one of us, the other was never too far away, but it just never happened that way. We were only twenty-four, and the gay market in Claremont wasn't exactly thriving. But we'd always missed the mark: dating other guys, nothing ever too permanent though, and never being single at the same time.

Until now.

"You sure you're okay?" he asked. I hadn't realised I'd zoned out again. "You were a million miles away. Either that or you really were checking out my arse."

I laughed him off and ignored how my cheeks heated. *Fuck.*

He studied me, a soft smile on his lips but a curious edge to his eyes. "I didn't think you were that serious about Shane. If you don't want to come away with me this weekend, just say so. I mean, you only broke up last weekend so—"

"I'm fine," I said, trying to brush off his concern. "I wasn't even thinking about him. We weren't that serious, just a couple of dates." He didn't look too convinced. "It's just work stuff, that's all. You know, you're right though. I do need this weekend away. Are you sure there's nothing you need me to grab?"

"Nah, we're good. I think I've got everything. Just bring yourself."

"Okay then. I'd better get going. See you at my place in the morning." I took a few steps out of the garage and down the driveway to my old truck.

"Hey Cal," Troy called out. He was standing there, holding a black piece of cloth and looking a little concerned. "Did you wanna hang out here a while? We can order something in to eat if you want?"

I wasn't my usual sarcastic self, and I knew he was concerned. So I gave him the best smile I could muster. "It's bad enough I have to put up with your ugly mug all weekend. No point in spoilin' my Thursday night too."

We were always taking the piss out of each other, so he must have been reassured I was okay because he grinned at me. "Yeah, I don't want to be interrupting your date with your *Hawaii Five-0* boyfriend. What's his name? Steve McGarrett?"

"That's Lieutenant Commander Steve McGarrett to you." I gave him a mock salute with my middle finger and mouthed "fuck you" as I got into my truck.

Troy just laughed and went back into his garage, and I drove away with a smile.

It was only a five-minute drive to my place. In a town of fifty-thousand people, it was only five minutes to anywhere. Just as I was pulling into the driveway, my phone rang. I fished it out of my pocket. It was Peta. I'd gotten to know her during my apprenticeship days, me a carpenter, her an electrician. Apprentices spent three days a week working, two days in the classroom, and we'd shared a table one day in the busy cafeteria, started up a conversation, and had been friends ever since. "Hey sparkie," I answered, knowing it would get a response from her.

"Hey chippie."

"How's things?"

"Good. Just seeing if you're still going away tomorrow?"

I cut the engine and got out of my truck and walked to my front door. "Yep. Why?"

"Did you need me to come by and feed Meggs?"

"Yeah, is that okay? If not, I can just leave food out for her. It's only two nights. I'm sure she'll be fine." I crooked the phone between my ear and shoulder so I could use both hands to unlock the door. Sometimes the front door stuck a little.

"Still haven't fixed your front door?"

"Shut up."

Peta laughed. "You know what they say: a carpenter's house is never finished, and a mechanic's car never runs right."

"An electrician's house is never wired right. Still have that ceiling fan that doesn't work?"

"Shut up."

I laughed and pushed my way inside and closed the door behind me with a hard shove.

"Speaking of mechanics," Peta said, and I suppressed a sigh. I knew what was coming. "Still just you and Troy going this weekend?"

"Yep. Robbo can't come. Christie has some family BBQ on." Paul Robertson, or Robbo as we called him, was a mate of ours. The three of us, and sometimes Allan and Mick, would usually do something on weekends. Our camping trips usually involved fishing, motorbike riding, and drinking beer.

Peta's voice through the phone interrupted my thoughts. "Well, I was talking to Christie today. She does have a family BBQ on. Her sister's in town, so that much is true."

I walked into my kitchen and threw my keys and wallet on the counter. "And?"

"Well, she also told Robbo not to go so you and Troy would finally have a weekend alone."

I let out a long sigh, allowed my head to fall forward and my shoulders to sag. "Peta," I started.

"Listen," she interrupted. "You need this. Everyone can see it except you two. And I'm telling you, he wants you as much you want him."

I scrubbed my hand over my face. I tried to reply, but I'd given up on this argument years ago. "He's my best mate. That's all."

"How long have you been in love with him?"

I swallowed hard.

"That's what I thought. You've got the whole weekend with him, Cal. Put yourself out there."

"And risk, what? Everything?"

Her voice was soft and resonating. "Wouldn't it be worth it?"

And for that I had no reply.

"Just think about it. I'm telling you, there's no way he'd say no."

"Look, I have to go."

"Calvin Lynch, you know I love you. I'm just telling you how it is." She always did. "I'll come around at lunch time and make sure Meggs is okay. And Cal?"

"Yeah?"

"I want all the details." I could tell she was smiling. "*All* of them."

"I'm going now."

"Say hello to Commander McGarrett for me."

I groaned into the phone and disconnected the call, cutting her laughter short. I wasn't that predictable, was I?

Meggs the cat sat perched on the arm of the sofa. She looked at me with such contempt, and I was certain if a cat could roll its eyes, she would. Her affections for me swayed between adoring and loathing, and I swear the only reason she tolerated me was because I fed her. She wasn't my cat. Not really. She came with the house, and I'd given her the name Ginger Meggs, given her colouring. As it turned out, he was a she, so we dropped the Ginger, and she just got Meggs.

I bought the house last year; a 'renovators dream' was the diplomatic way of calling it a dump. It was an old three-bedroom weatherboard in a pretty good part of town, but the house had good bones. Given I was a builder by trade, I had plans to do it up as time and finances allowed.

I planted myself on the sofa with a heavy sigh, and picking up the remote, I turned the TV on just as *Hawaii Five-0* was just about to start. It was perfect timing really. Meggs decided she'd grace me with her presence and curled up on my lap.

"It's not my fault Steve McGarrett's hot," I said to Meggs. It also wasn't my fault he reminded me of Troy. Peta's conversation echoed in my mind. "Fuck."

Meggs never replied. Not that I expected her to. Not that I needed her to. I already knew the answer.

I was screwed either way. Damned if I did, damned if I didn't. Was risking my friendship with my best friend worth it? God, what if he said no? What if he laughed in my face? Ugh. I couldn't do it. I wouldn't.

…but butterflies took off in my belly because, well, what if he said yes?

CHAPTER TWO

WHEN TROY ARRIVED at my place at six o'clock, I threw my gear into the back and climbed into his ute. His ute was his pride and joy, in pristine condition, immaculate inside and out. It was rigged with every 4x4 off-roader gadget on the market, and as a mechanic, what was under the hood was perfect too.

I handed him an egg and bacon burger and slid his coffee into his cup holder. Before he could argue, I said, "If any spills, I'll detail the interior myself."

He just smiled. "Thanks."

I knew he was meticulous about his ute, and that was fine with me. He was proud of it, and he should be. He'd worked hard for everything he had.

He started to drive out of town, heading for the mountains. There were other, more popular recreational dams we could have gone to, but given it was a long weekend, they'd be packed with families and kids. Troy had done some work for a guy who owned some property about an hour and a half out of town, right up the top of the hills that ran east of Claremont. The property had a river that had been stocked with trout, and in what was a fair trade, Troy did a free service on the guy's car for a few weekends throughout the year of free fishing. It was perfect really.

I unwrapped his burger for him and handed it to him. He took it graciously. "Did you make these?"

"Yep," I answered. "Yours is egg, bacon, and BBQ sauce. Coffee is white with one."

Troy grinned at me, then he bit into his burger and spoke with his mouth full. "Mmm, it's good."

We ate in silence as he drove, and when he put half his burger on his lap, I handed him his coffee. "Thanks," he said with a warm smile. He took a mouthful and handed it back to me. I put it in his cup holder for him, ignoring how our fingers brushed, ignoring how we did things that couples did... ignoring how my heart tripped over and how butter-flies set my stomach on edge.

"Hey, weren't we supposed to get ice at the servo?" I asked, just remembering that he'd said that yesterday.

"Already got it," he answered, swallowing down the last of his breakfast. "I was up early, so I filled up on fuel and grabbed some ice before I got to your place this morning."

Oh. "Let me know what I owe you for that."

"Forget about it. You paid for all the food."

I shrugged. It was true. Our weekends away fishing usually squared off with each other. One of us would pay for one thing, the other would pay for something else. It was no big deal either way.

I stretched out as much as I could and took Troy's phone out of the cradle on the dash. "You right there?" he asked with a smile.

"Yep," I answered, thumbing the screen. "You need to update your playlists."

He chuckled, that deep familiar rumble I'd know anywhere. "You know, technology's great, but I miss the days of car stereos with CDs. Then I could just keep one CD, and you'd have to like it or lump it."

"And you'd make that one and only CD some country shit too."

Troy laughed. "Damn straight."

I scrolled through his playlists. "Jesus, man. Do you have any music that doesn't have a steel guitar?"

"Not any worth playing."

I recradled his phone and took out my own. I'd set up my phone to connect to Bluetooth in Troy's ute the first time I got in it. Because that's what best friends did: they rode shotgun, and they directed the music. I disconnected his phone, connected mine, and opted for random. Because seriously, any song on my phone was better than his.

"Make yourself at home," Troy said. The corner of his lips twitched with a well-fought smile.

I leaned my head back and closed my eyes. "I always do."

He only got through half a song. "And you think my taste in music is shit."

"Yes, yes I do."

"This is crap. All these new so-called singers aren't even musicians. I bet half of 'em couldn't even play the guitar or piano."

"Is that the catalyst of what makes a musician?"

"It should be."

"What if they're a drummer?"

"Drummers are acceptable. These tossers you listen to only know how to press buttons on a synthesiser. If they had to play a live concert with an actual band, they wouldn't know how."

I snorted out a laugh. "And your country twangers would have to put their banjos down so they could brush their one and only tooth with a toothbrush they share with their cousin."

Troy laughed. "What's wrong with a banjo?"

"The one tooth and toothbrush-sharing cousin doesn't bother you?"

He shook his head and laughed. "Just listen to your shit music and shut up."

———

WHEN TROY PULLED onto the dirt road, I jumped out of the ute to open the gate. He drove through and I shut the gate behind him, and when I got back into his ute, Troy was smiling.

I knew that smile. It was his gone-fishin' smile, his "weekend away with no mobile phone service" smile. Possibly even his "Friday night footy and pizza" smile. It was contagious.

The property we were on was a two-hundred-acre lot, mostly hilly with overgrown vegetation. It wasn't good for much else than fishing and goats. Apparently the owners bought it a few years back, intending to put a weekender on it, but I liked that there was no house on it. I liked that it was secluded. For me, that was the very best part.

The dirt road meandered through overgrown outcrops around the side of a hill, and we followed it down to the river. There was a spot levelled off not far from the water where we usually made camp, and the circle of rocks in the front still held charcoal evidence of the last time we'd been here.

Troy stopped the ute just to the back of the campsite and got out, stretching his hands high above his head with a smile. His shirt rode up, revealing that dark trail of hair, which ran from his navel down past the waistband of his—

"You getting out of the ute? Or you gonna fish from there?"

I flipped him off and got out of the ute. The sound of the water and the feel of sunlight on my skin made me smile. "We setting up camp? Or seeing if they're biting first?"

Troy scoffed out a laugh and reached up to unscrew the cap on the fishing-rod holder. "Whadda you think?"

I smiled to myself. It really was a stupid question. "I'll get the flies."

WE WALKED upstream to find a deeper pocket of water and stood on the riverbank about fifteen metres apart. We rarely spoke, and when we did it was just a quiet murmur or a simple nod. It was always quiet, the only sounds around us was the water, crickets chirping, and birds singing. The sun was warm on my skin, and the repetitive feed of fishing line flicking out over the water was something I could feel soothing out my tangled mind.

I had to admit, as much as I enjoyed fishing, watching Troy was even better. He stood on the bank, casting the line back and forth fluidly. His right arm and shoulder flexed, the muscles bunching and sliding with every graceful movement. He was wearing footy shorts and an old T-shirt that he'd had forever; his baseball cap melded perfectly to the shape of his head. He might have looked nothing special to a lot of other people—a little too rugged and casual for most other gay blokes in town—but he sure looked fine to me. And then he'd smile at me in the sunshine.

Yep, fly fishing with Troy was one of my favourite things.

It was peaceful being here with him. Sometimes when the other fellas came with us, it was fun and always good for a laugh. But when it was just me and Troy, it was so easy. There were no awkward silences, no pressure to fill any void in conversation. We simply liked each other's company. I mean, sometimes he'd come to my place to just hang out on the couch like he owned it, or I'd go to his place and hand him tools and stuff while he was fine tuning the engine of his ute. We didn't have to speak. We just had to be in each other's company.

A sudden flick out of the corner of my eye caught my

attention, followed by a splash in the water. "Woah," Troy said, winding the reel in furiously.

"Oh you are kidding me," I cried. "We haven't even been here for an hour!"

Troy just laughed as he fought the fish, giving it line, then reeling it in a little bit more each time. I reeled my line in, still shaking my head. "Every damn time. You catch something first, every damn time."

Troy landed the trout onto the bank. It was a nice looking fish, decent size and healthy. "I have skills," he said with a laugh. He picked up the fish and posed with it like a photo, big, cheesy grin and all.

"You suck."

"Yes. Yes, I do. Very well too, or so I've been told."

I snorted out a laugh, despite not wanting to think about the guys who'd been in his bed when I hadn't. When he'd chosen them and not me…

Troy walked over to me, holding his fish. "Jeez Cal, you look like someone stole your last dollar. Is that because of the dick-sucking joke? Or because I caught the first fish. Again?"

I gave his shoulder a hard shover. "Fuck you."

He replied with a laugh. "I caught it, you can gut and clean it."

"Piss off. You know the rule, you catch it, you clean it."

"I just worked hard to catch your dinner tonight. It's the least you can do." He led the way along the river back to camp, and I followed with a rather pleasant view of his back and arse. "You know, like the dinner rule. I cook, you clean."

"When have you ever cooked me dinner?"

"I bring pizza. It's technically the same thing."

"Oh bullshit. Cooking dinner for someone is a three course meal."

"I'll cook a three course meal tonight," he said proudly. "The fish, and two beers. That's three courses, right?"

I laughed at that. "Well, according to you it is."

"Okay, I'll make a deal with you. I'll make you a three course dinner."

"Pizza, garlic bread, and beer doesn't count."

He snorted. "Damn. No, for real. A proper three course meal. Entrée, main, and dessert. Next weekend."

"What's the catch?"

"No catch. Well, just the dinner rule. I cook, you clean."

"Gee. Thanks."

"Then you have to do the same for me. And I have high expectations, just so you know."

"So it's like the *MasterChef* finale."

"More like the *Iron Chef* finale. You get to pick the ingredients that I have to cook for you, and then I pick the ingredients for what you have to cook for me. Only without the really bad English voices dubbed over the Japanese ones."

"You watch far too much television."

He grinned over his shoulder at me. "Only if you include porn. Which reminds me, I need to check when my subscription is up for renewal."

I barked out a laugh. "God forbid it runs out."

"Well, we can't all have a line of guys waiting in turn like you do."

I stopped walking. "I do not."

He turned around, and if he was concerned by my offended look, he didn't let on. He just grinned even wider. "Oh Cal. Please don't act like you're oblivious."

"You're so full of shit." I walked toward him and gave him another shove as I walked past him. He just laughed and easily caught up to me. We walked back to the campsite and were side by side as we neared the ute. I was still grumbling under my breath, and he was still smiling.

Troy wrapped the fish and put it in the Esky of ice. He clapped his hands together. "Come on then, Mister one-boyfriend-after-the-next. You're helping me with the tent."

"What? No pitching tent jokes?"

"I'm not twelve. Besides, erections while camping isn't a laughing matter. It's intents."

I blinked, he waited.

"Get it? *In tents.*"

I sighed, but ended up laughing anyway. "That was so not funny."

"Then why are you laughing?"

"Because you're an idiot."

He grinned at me, and we went about setting up the tent. It was supposedly big enough to sleep six people, but unless those six people were all under the age of five, I would doubt it very much.

I unrolled my air mattress and attached the connector, when I noticed Troy looking at me. "You can't be serious."

Now I grinned at him. "Hell yes."

"If Robbo and Mick were here, they'd take the piss for years."

"I only brought it because I knew they wouldn't be here," I explained. "And anyway, it beats sleeping on the ground or in a swag. And it's a double so you can sleep on it too."

"With you?"

"Yeah, why? Is that such a terrible thought?" I asked, half joking, half not. "Because according to you, there's a line of guys who would kill for the chance."

Troy choked out a laugh and his cheeks tinted pink. It wasn't quite the reaction I was expecting. "No, it's fine." He cleared his throat and pulled the sleeping bags off the back of the ute. "Just wasn't expecting a proposition from you, that's all."

I stared at him. "It wasn't... I didn't..." *Fuck.* "That wasn't what I meant."

He gave me a tight smile, one so unlike him that it threw me. He threw the sleeping bags inside the tent and then pulled the other crates off the back of his ute. The tight edge of his jaw and narrowed eyes told me he obviously no longer wanted to talk. *Bloody hell.* I started the small air compressor and watched the air mattress fill with air. When it was done, I pulled it into the tent and rolled my sleeping bag out on it but stopped when I picked up Troy's.

Did he want to sleep on it with me? I had no clue and certainly wasn't going to ask. I unrolled and laid it out next to mine, figuring if he didn't want to share the mattress with me, he could go ahead and sleep on the fucking ground.

I climbed out of the tent and found Troy setting up the grill. "I'll just go grab some firewood," I said. I didn't wait for him to reply, I just started off for the line of trees. I guess the bit of space and time would do us good.

We were never like this. We never *not* talked, and things were never tense like this. He's never cared about which guys I dated before, so why bring it up now? I had to wonder what was different, when Peta's words came back to me.

He's into you, Cal. He'd never say no to you.

My feet stopped and I almost stumbled. No, surely not. I mean, I've always been the one who was in love with him, not the other way around, right?

Oh God. This put a whole new level of tension between us. If that's what this was.

I had to tell my feet to keep moving because if Troy saw me standing still in the middle of the clearing, he'd ask me what the hell I was doing, and I wasn't ready to talk about this. Not yet. I needed time to process, maybe read some more signs. It wasn't like I could stomp back over to him and demand to know the truth. I mean, what if I was wrong? What if he laughed at me? What if he thought I thought he wanted me and that made me a conceited jerk? What if—

"What if what?"

I spun around, holding a stick. "What?"

Troy laughed. "You were taking so long I thought I'd come over and see what was up. Turns out you were just waving half a branch around mumbling to yourself."

I looked at the stick. "It's hardly half a branch."

"Well, I wondered whether you were sizing it up for a quidditch match. It's too small to be a broomstick, too big for a wand."

I groaned. Again with the Harry Potter jokes. I'd mistakenly suggested to him we should re-enact a quidditch match and he was never going to let me live that down. "I was in high school!"

He laughed. "And totally in love with Harry."

I sighed and let my shoulders sag. "I regret ever telling you that."

"Having fantasies about fictional characters is completely normal. Acting out on them is a little weird."

"Fuck you. And suggesting a real live quidditch match is hardly fantasising. I told you back then it would be a bit like European handball mixed with AFL and hockey. It would have been awesome."

"Sure. If you're a wizard, that is." His eyes were alight with humour and a smile teased his lips.

I was just glad we were back to our normal selves, and I found myself smiling back at him. "And anyway," I added. "You just didn't want to play because I would have kicked your arse."

He scoffed. "Not likely."

I picked up some more fallen sticks and small branches. "Yes likely. And I was never *in love* with Harry. I was like twelve years old. It was a mild childhood infatuation."

Troy roared laughing. "Oh, that's a good one. I should write that down."

"To explain your mild childhood infatuation with Take That?"

He put his hand to his heart. "You wound me."

"But it proves one thing. That you've never really had good taste in music."

He just laughed. "But then I found Keith Urban."

"And I've paid dearly for that discovery. Years of country music. It's like a form of aural torture."

His wide gaze shot to mine.

"I said aural, not oral."

"Phew," he said, wiping his brow. "I thought for a second there you had some weird kink I didn't know about."

I laughed at that and, shaking my head, picked up some more wood. "Nope. No kinks."

"None?" he asked. "That's a little disappointing. I thought for sure you had some huge dildo collection. Because I've seen—"

"You've seen my dildo—?"

He roared laughing. "No, I haven't. But you just gave yourself away, so bad. Oh my God, that's a classic."

"Remind me why we're friends?"

"Because I'm awesome."

"I'm questioning my judgement in friends right now."

"Not your judgement in dildos?" He was trying not to laugh. "Or you got that down to an art?"

"Oh hell yes, I do. My personal favourite is the eight inch ribbed with prostate wand. Best orgasm of your life, every time, guaranteed."

He wasn't laughing now. In fact, his mouth fell open, his eyes wide, and the stick he was holding now hung limp in his hand. He blinked slowly, speechless.

I burst out laughing, turned on my heel, and headed back to camp. "That's what I thought."

Troy ran to catch up with me. "You're serious?" He cleared his throat. "I mean I've never... never mind, this is really embarrassing."

I dropped my armful of firewood near the campfire. "Don't be embarrassed. I just said it to shut you up because you were taking the piss. But yes, it is my favourite, yes it will be the best sex you've ever had, and yes, I can order you one online when we get back in the land of Wi-Fi."

He scrubbed his hand over his face. "Okay, this conversation isn't happening."

I clapped my hand on the top of his arm. "You're welcome." This was the most we'd ever talked about sex before. We talked about everything else, but nothing about our sex lives. It was just always a topic we kept private. I didn't want to hear of his conquests and what he did with them. And he must have felt the same because in all the years we'd known each other, he'd never brought it up either. So yes, this was new for us, and I didn't want him to freak out any more than he already was. "Want me to fix you some lunch? I packed some roast beef for sandwiches."

He looked hopeful. "Got any of your mum's pickles?"

"Of course."

CHAPTER THREE

WE FISHED ALL AFTERNOON. This time we walked farther up to where the river broadened, and we stood knee-deep in the water about thirty metres apart. I wasn't sure if I caught him looking at me every so often or if it was me who got caught looking at him.

But he'd look away all shy-like, and it did stupid things to my heartbeat. I spent the entire time mechanically throwing out my line and slowly reeling it back in, not thinking a single thought about fishing.

My mind was stuck on Troy.

We'd spent our entire dating lives out of sync. When he was single, I was seeing someone else and vice versa. There was never really a time when we were single at the same time, until now. Actually, he'd been single for a while, and I'd just broken up with Shane. Not that I was ever serious about Shane. I mean, he was a nice guy, but we weren't truly compatible. We'd fooled around a little, and after 'dating' for about a month, we still hadn't had sex. I wasn't that into him, and when he asked if it was a step I'd consider taking some point soon, I declined and he bailed.

Troy never really liked him, and that was a turn off for me. If the guy I was seeing didn't like my friends or if they didn't like him, I wasn't seeing him for much longer. I knew where my loyalties lay: mates before dates, always. Sure, like Troy said I'd had a string of boyfriends, but none of them were ever around for too long. There was Ryan, who last year I'd seen for about six months, but he just wasn't… I don't know. He wasn't what I was looking for.

He wasn't Troy.

Suddenly he was beside me. "Are you trying to solve an algebra equation in your head, or you trying to fart?"

I hadn't heard him come over. His question made me laugh. "What?"

"That look on your face," he said, smiling broadly. "It's either maths or gas."

I barked out a laugh. "I take it the fish aren't biting for you either?"

"Nah. Wanna call it a day?"

"Yep." I reeled in my line, hooking the fly up to an eyelet on the rod. He was staring at my fingers. "You alright?"

"Yeah, yeah," he said, wading his way to the riverbank. "Suppose I better get that dinner started."

I followed him back to camp, where he scaled and gutted the fish, and I got the fire started. Then I put together some bread and salad while he cooked. We were like a left and right hand. We worked autonomously, we moved around each other with a familiarity I'd never known with anyone else.

I held up the two plates, and he slid a portion of fish onto each one. I handed him his, and we sat back in front of the fire and ate in a peaceful, easy silence. The sun was getting ready to call it a day, the horizon a spray of oranges and blues. The evening was warm, crickets and birds were telling bedtime stories, and Troy smiled as he sipped his beer.

It was pretty fucking perfect.

"Everything at work okay?" he asked.

"Yeah. Why wouldn't it be?"

"The other day you were distracted and said something was up at work." Troy picked at the label on his beer bottle. "Thought it might be you breaking up with Shane."

Oh, shit. That's right. I was in his garage wondering if he could ever possibly see me as more than a friend when he'd asked me if I was okay. I'd lied and told him it was work. "Work's okay. And things with me and Shane…" I didn't know how to finish that sentence.

"Things with you and Shane were what?" he pressed. I shrugged, and he took a swig of beer. "I thought you and him were good."

I shook my head. "He's a nice guy."

"Just nice?"

I gave him a smile. "He was a decent guy. Meant well."

"But?"

But he wasn't you.

"But he just wasn't for me."

"Didn't have some weird sex fetish you weren't into?" he asked jokingly, but there was a tightness in his eyes.

I laughed. "Wouldn't know. Didn't get that far."

Troy's eyebrows shot up before he could school his features. "Oh."

"Yeah, like I said, he just wasn't for me."

He studied me for a scrutinising moment. "You okay? You've been a bit quiet lately, a bit out of sorts."

Should I tell him? Could I? I stared at him, trying to push the air out of my lungs to speak. I had no clue what words I would say… Should it be this hard? Was I risking too much? We both sat there, across the fire from each other and stared at one another for what felt like forever. His gaze was intense, and I swear he saw into my very soul.

He broke the connection between us, looking at the fire

instead. He swallowed hard and let out a steady breath. "You don't have to tell me," he said quietly.

"It's not that," I replied lamely. "I dunno. Just lonely, I guess."

His head jerked up, his gaze fixed on my eyes. "Yeah?"

I had to look away this time. My heart was hammering, and my stomach was in knots. I wasn't ready for this conversation, was I? Instead of manning up, instead of telling him the truth, I laughed it off. "Sick of dating strangers. Sick of the whole getting-to-know-someone phase, treading-on-eggshells phase, only to find out they're not—" *you* "—what I'm after. People say the dating scene is fun and exciting, but it's not. It's tiring and disappointing."

He gave me a half smile before looking back at his beer. "Then you're dating the wrong guys."

I barked out a laugh, because that was the understatement of the fucking century. "It's a pain in the arse."

"Then you're not using enough lube."

I stared at him before shaking my head and laughing despite my sullen mood. "I'll keep that in mind."

The seriousness to our conversation was over, and the rest of the night passed with us talking shit about football, the local gossip, and general bullshit. When it came time to go to bed, I'd forgotten I'd suggested we share a mattress.

Troy had gone to take a piss, and I stripped down to my undies and climbed into my sleeping bag. When he came back into the tent, he balked at the bed. "Oh, that's right. You princessed up and brought along an airbed."

I rolled onto my side and snuggled down into my sleeping bag, pulling my pillow under my head, pretending not to notice him get undressed. "It beats the hell out of sleeping on the ground. Which, by the way, you're more than welcome to do."

"Hell no," he said, quickly climbing into his sleeping bag.

Once he was settled, he sighed. "Okay, so this was a good idea. Just don't tell the others."

I chuckled. "You're welcome."

Troy yawned. "Early start's catching up with me. Slept like shit last night."

He'd mentioned he was up earlier than normal. "Something on your mind?"

He was quiet for a second. "Yeah," he mumbled. "Sleeping."

It wasn't long until his breathing evened out. He was flat on his back, and there was enough moonlight for me to see his lips slightly parted; his eyelashes fanned across his cheeks. He looked peaceful and even more gorgeous than he did in the daylight. His chest rose and fell with his deep breaths, and I let myself pretend he was mine. I imagined we were in my bed back home and this was just a normal night. I longed to touch him, to have him touch me in return. I wanted him, but more than that, I wanted him to want me. I ached for it.

I pulled my pillow down again and rolled a little toward him, but I wanted more. Then I crossed the line. I pretended to be asleep and rolled into his side. I kept my eyes closed and perfectly still, hoping he wouldn't wake and push me away. My heart was thundering and my chest burned; I was touching him. Though it wasn't real, it wasn't reciprocated, but it was everything I craved.

Then Troy rolled over, put his arm around me, and tucked me into his neck. He mumbled something sleepily, incoherently, and I was frozen. Maybe I should have pushed him away. Maybe I should have moved as far back as I could. But this, *this* was what I needed.

He was warmth and Old Spice. His arm around me was perfection. And I knew, I knew in my heart, there would never be anyone else for me. This is what I longed for. He was what was missing from my life.

I just had to tell him.

I told myself I'd think about that later. Right now, I was in heaven. I resisted the urge to touch him back. He was sleeping, after all. But I sure as hell could enjoy the feel of his arm around me. So I did. I lay there until I fell asleep, wrapped in the arms of a man I loved and would probably never get to have.

CHAPTER FOUR

I WOKE up to find Troy's sleeping bag empty. It was just starting to get light outside, so I had to wonder if he was getting ready for an early fish or if he'd woken up beside me and freaked out.

God, was I still snuggled into him? Was he horrified? Did he think I was some kind of joke? Would he take the piss outta me? I scrubbed my hands over my face. Last night felt like a different reality. I'd needed to feel him close last night; I'd let him put his arm around me, and I pretended like it meant something. And now, in the cold light of a new day, I felt like a fool.

And worse than that, I knew now I had to tell him.

Because, even if it turned out Troy would not, or could not, ever be interested in me, it was too late for me. I was in love with him. I had been for years. Was I supposed to risk it all? Was I supposed to tell him how I felt? Because it was getting to the point where I couldn't keep pretending I wasn't in love with my best friend. I didn't have a choice anymore. I had to either tell him or walk away.

And I couldn't be the one to say goodbye.

I climbed out of the sleeping bag, pulled on some shorts,

and got out of the tent, putting both hands up to yawn and stretch the kinks out of my back. "Ah, sleeping beauty," Troy said. He was to my left, sitting in the first rays of sunlight holding one moth-like fishing fly expertly between his fingers. I turned to face him, and his eyes raked over my shirtless torso and dropped to my dick. He stared, his mouth slightly open, his cheeks tinged pink. Fuck, I've never seen that look on his face before…

Realising I had a semi, I coughed and grabbed my half morning wood. "I need to take a piss," I said. "Don't judge." I walked off in the opposite direction to the first line of trees and relieved myself, trying not to think about the look of want on his face. God, he looked like he wanted to drop to his knees and suck me right then and there. And that didn't exactly make peeing easy. In fact, my half morning wood was becoming full wood, and that would make everything worse. By the time I got myself back under control by remembering I was going to tell him I was in love with him and he was going to laugh and tell me I was a dickhead, I went back to find him waiting for me, fishing rods in hand.

He held mine out to me. "Thought you got lost," he said. He was smiling. The look of desire from before was long gone. "Come on or the fish'll know we're coming."

"Let me grab a shirt," I said, quickly ducking into the tent. I couldn't be sure, but I thought it sounded like he mumbled, "Feel free not to". When I came back out, he'd already started to walk downstream this time. The river changed its course a little this way, only steep river banks and deeper pools of still water instead of wide and flat with rapids and shallows. Troy obviously decided that was where the fish were today, and I always took his lead when it came to fishing. I grabbed my fishing rod, pulled on my sneakers, and caught up to him easily.

"What about breakfast?" I asked as we walked the riverbank.

"Don't worry, you can cook it when we get back."

I laughed. "Gee, thanks."

"Anytime. I think I'll have sausages today, though, not bacon."

"Oh, for fuck sake," I said on a sigh. "It was morning wood, and I needed to pee."

Troy stopped walking and turned to look at me. He was obviously confused for a split second before he realised I thought he was taking the piss about my grand entrance from the tent, parading off my half-hard dick. He roared laughing. "No," he choked out. "I actually meant *actual* sausages. Not *your* sausage. Oh my God," he wheezed as he laughed some more. "That is the funniest thing I've ever heard."

"Oh fuck you," I said, walking past him and giving his shoulder a shove. "You totally checked me out this morning. If you want to eat my dick, you just have to ask."

Well, he wasn't laughing now, and I realised what I'd just said. See? I could say these things to him as a joke, but any hint of seriousness about how I felt, and I froze with fear. I didn't dare look behind me, I just kept on walking. I wasn't sure what to make of his silence, but I could hear him still following me, so it wasn't a complete loss.

I stopped at a nice spot, right above a deep trough in the river. There was a fallen log and reeds, and it was a perfect hiding hole for hungry trout. "This is me," I said.

Troy walked past me with a smile. "Still can't believe you said that. And I can't believe no one else was here to hear it. You're lucky the other guys aren't here, or they'd never let you live it down."

"And you will?"

His answer was just a laugh as he kept on walking. I shook my head, more at myself than him, and sat my arse on the riverbank. Troy chose a spot about thirty metres from me. There were a few trees between us, but I could see and hear him just fine. Our before-breakfast fishing bouts usually only lasted for about an hour or until someone's stomach rumbles started to frighten the fish. Today it was mine. It was about seven o'clock, and my stomach wouldn't wait any longer. "I'm heading back," I called out. "I'll start breakfast."

He grinned at me, and I knew it was coming.

"Remember, I want sausage this morning."

Aaaand there it was. "Yeah, lemme guess. Eight inches and thick."

He put his hand to his heart. "You know me so well."

I was still smiling to myself when he came back to camp. I figured the smell of breakfast cooking wouldn't keep him gone long. I had sausages, eggs and fried tomato, and bread toasted on the open fire. "Man, this smells so good," he said, planting himself right next to me.

I dished his up and handed it to him, then mine, and we ate in silence. Well, apart from the indecent moans and the occasional "this is so good" coming from Troy as he ate everything in sight. Afterwards, he leaned back and rubbed his belly. "You cook a damn good brekky. I can't decide if I need to go for a run or go back to bed."

I looked at him with one raised eyebrow. "Wow. And not even one sausage joke."

He grinned. "I was being mature."

"No you weren't. You just didn't want me to offer for you to suck my dick because you want it."

He laughed again, but he blushed. This was new from him, this embarrassment when we talked shit with each other. Or maybe I was just noticing it now that Peta had mentioned it to me? Because that look on his face right now was yes, yes he did want to suck my dick.

Jesus. I thought my blood caught fire. I felt warm all over, and he was so close. I wasn't even sure if I still managed to breathe.

Troy shot to his feet and grabbed my plate. "You cooked, I'll clean," he said, then busied himself with boiling some water on the fire to wash up with. "Let me know if the fish are biting."

Okay then. He obviously needed some space.

"No problem," I replied. I aimed for cheerful but didn't know how it came out. Probably strained, at best. I went back to the spot I was in earlier and parked my arse on the river-bank again. I cast the line out once and just left it, because my mind was certainly not on fishing. At all.

Holy shit.

There was definitely some tension between me and Troy. Good tension, sexual tension. I'd never picked up on his nervousness before. I don't actually think he was ever nervous around me like that before. But that look on his face, that heat in his eyes... I recognised that look. He'd just never aimed it at me before. But I couldn't deny it, he certainly aimed it at me now. I wasn't imagining it. I wasn't seeing something that wasn't there.

Holy shit.

I think Peta was right. I think Troy could want me too.

I got to my feet and was just about to reel my line in and go demand an answer from him, when he walked past. He had his rod in hand and wore a tight smile and kept a very obvious distance between us. If he were any further off the track, he'd be in the trees.

Okay then, maybe not.

"Any luck?" he asked. He didn't even stop, he just kept walking.

Well, that was a loaded question. "No. None."

He took his spot downstream from me and stood on the bank. He flicked the line out several times, slowly and expertly. And he never said another thing to me.

I looked at him a couple of times and caught him shaking his head and mumbling to himself once or twice, the way he does when he's pissed off.

Something was definitely up, and I was pretty sure we were going to be dealing with it today.

I put my rod beside me and laid back on the grass. It was peaceful here—the sounds of the water and the birds—but this new tension between me and Troy put me off kilter. I closed my eyes and tried to centre myself, but somewhere along the way, I must have fallen asleep.

A huge clap of thunder woke me, and quite frankly, scared the bajeesus outta me. "Holy fuck!" I cried, clambering to my feet.

Then in sync, Troy and I both looked up at the sky, just as the heavens opened. I grabbed my rod and bolted back to camp, knowing Troy would be right behind me.

We moved what we could out of the rain and went for cover inside the tent, Troy followed close behind me. I sat on my sleeping bag and pulled my now-wet shoes off and lay them near the door, then pulled off my shirt. I shook my head, much like a wet dog, and laughed, but when I looked over at Troy, he wasn't laughing. He was kneeling beside me—there wasn't much room in the tent for him to be anywhere else—and he was dripping wet. He was breathing hard and his eyes were narrowed.

In fact, he still looked kinda pissed off.

"What's up?" I asked. "It's just a bit of water."

He said nothing.

"Did you check the weather forecast?" I asked, changing the subject. He said nothing, but his eyes were focused on my mouth and he licked his lips. I swallowed hard. "Just wondered how long it's gonna rain, that's all."

With a look of pure determination, Troy grabbed hold of my face and kissed me. I was surprised and he was off balance, and we kinda fell apart. He recoiled and looked horrified. "I'm sorry," he whispered. He looked about ready to bolt outside into the rain, but I snatched the shirt at his chest and fisted it tight.

His gaze met mine, a mix of uncertainty and longing. I brought my other hand up to his cheek, touching him as if he were made of glass. I leaned in slowly, his breath hitched and his eyes fluttered closed, and just before our lips met, I stopped. This moment, I'd waited years for this... I took everything in. His face, the smell of him in the rain, his pink lips so close to mine, and that nervous, heart-stopping almost-kiss perfect moment.

Then I pressed my lips to his. It was tender at first; the rough feel of his stubble combined with the softness of his mouth was a heady mix. His scent, his taste... I had to remind myself this was Troy. My best friend. Then I had to remind myself to breathe.

I pulled back a little, and we both drew a breath. I never let go of shirt, I kept him right where he was; our faces just an inch apart.

"I've wanted to do that for so long," he murmured breathlessly. He looked drunk. I smiled and pulled him in for another kiss. Only this time, I leaned back on the airbed and brought him with me. He fell on top of me, and he pulled back a little. "Cal?"

I ran my hands through his hair and over his face, down his jaw, taking in the closeness of his mouth. "I've wanted you since I was fourteen." I stared at his lips and whispered, "You kissed me."

He settled his weight on me and encased my face in his hands. "I tried to fight it. But then you were wet."

I chuckled, and a crack of thunder boomed over us. It seemed to add to the static between us. "Don't fight it. I don't want to fight this anymore."

This time he kissed me properly, tilting his head and opening my lips with his own. He slid his tongue against mine, and I thought my heart might stop. I opened my legs wider and he bucked his hips. I could feel his erection, hot and hard against mine, and I moaned without shame. It made Troy shiver, and that made me smile.

Troy pulled back, a smile playing at his lips too. I slid my hands down his sides and over his arse, pulling him against me. His eyes rolled back before they closed. "Cal," he murmured.

I gripped his face and his eyes shot open. "Say my name again," I demanded.

He barely breathed the word. "Cal."

In all the years I'd known him, he'd never said my name like that. "Fuck." I brought his mouth to mine again, kissing him for all I was worth. And by God, he could kiss. He rolled his hips into mine, over and over, our cocks rubbing deliciously together. And I couldn't help it. I needed more. I needed… everything.

I slipped my hand between us and palmed him the best I could. He shuddered against me and stopped. He stopped moving, he stopped kissing me. "Cal, you're gonna make me come."

And that was music to my ears. I slid my hand under the elastic waistband of his footy shorts and wrapped my fingers around his shaft. He was hot and hard in my hand, but the angle was awkward and I couldn't grip him properly. So I pulled his shorts down over his arse and fumbled, trying to get them off him. He rolled off me and pulled them down himself, tossing them toward the opening flap of the tent.

I pounced on him, landing between his legs this time. He laughed and gripped my hips as I kissed him again, pushing him into the airbed. His hard cock lay up toward his belly, and God I wanted it. I freed my cock and, taking us both in my hand, rubbed our erections together.

Holy shit! I'd never felt anything like it. Not with anyone else had it felt this good. Our cocks slid together, like silk over hot steel. We were slick with precome, sliding and rutting, and he had his hands all over me. In my hair, down my back, over my arse. His mouth was on mine, his tongue in my mouth. He was everywhere, and it still wasn't enough.

It would never be enough.

But then his hips jerked underneath me, his cock pulsed in my hand. He dug his blunt fingernails into my back, and I got to watch pure bliss in his eyes as he came.

He arched his back and his cock surged before spilling come between us. And it was so hot, so perfect, and so fucking good, that I followed right after him.

I collapsed on top of him, both of our chests heaving, our breaths ragged. But I refused to let things get weird between us. I refused to let him freak out. I rolled us onto our sides and pulled a sleeping bag over us and kissed him softly. "Thank you," I said. I felt sleepy and the most content I'd ever felt.

"What for?" he asked gruffly.

"For taking a chance. For kissing me first."

He smiled tiredly, his eyes were heavy-lidded. "You know, this air mattress was a really good idea."

I laughed and pulled him closer, kissing him again. "We're a bit of a mess."

"Clean up later," he mumbled, snuggling into me, clearly with no intention of moving.

I kissed the side of his head. "After round two."

I felt him smile against my neck, and the storm rolled on outside.

CHAPTER FIVE

I DOZED FOR A LITTLE WHILE. The orgasm-induced haze and sound of rain on the tent, and of course having Troy in my arms, made for perfect dozing. He stirred and his hold on me tightened. "Tell me I'm not dreaming," he mumbled.

"You're not dreaming." I kissed the side of his head. "Never had you pegged as the type to sleep after sex."

His response was half a chuckle, half "Fuck off."

I sighed contentedly. "So this is new."

He smiled. "It is. And it's not. I mean, it's been about eight years in the making."

I pulled back and waited for him to look at me. I kissed his lips. "I thought it was just me."

Troy shook his head. "I nearly told you so many times, but it was never the right time. And I didn't know what to say anyway."

"Me too."

"Remember that time in our senior year, the day I got my first car?" I nodded and he continued, "I picked you up, and it was like the best day ever, and we drove all around town and down to the river and I was gonna tell you then. I was so close. I almost said it, but you told me you were hooking up with Philip Easley."

"You remember his name?"

His eyes flickered with something I couldn't quite name. "Of course I do. I was trying to work up the courage to kiss you when you told me that."

"Oh."

"And then there was that time when I got my apprenticeship and we got some beers…"

"And I was seeing Damien." I closed my eyes. "It wasn't just me, you know. I wanted to tell you a thousand times too. But we were never in sync. One of us was always seeing someone else."

His hand on my face made me look at him. His voice was so quiet, so unsure. "Are we in sync now?"

I nodded. "Yeah." I pressed my lips to his. "Finally."

He smiled, the eye crinkling kind of smile. "Finally."

"You know Peta told me the reason why none of the other guys came with us this weekend was so we'd be alone," I said. "Apparently everyone knew but us, and thought we needed a push."

"We did need a push." He traced his thumb along my eyebrow. "God, I can't believe I'm touching you like this."

"Surreal, huh?" I kissed him again. Now that I could kiss him after so many years of fantasising about it, I didn't ever want to stop. "Doesn't sound like that rain is gonna ease up anytime soon."

"Good," he replied, rolling me onto my back. He kissed me, deeper, with more purpose and passion, holding my face and tilting my head so he could kiss me deeper still. I opened my legs, and he settled on top of me. Feeling every inch of him, being kissed—being owned—by him, turned my bones to sponge.

I loved the feel of his weight on me. We fit together so perfectly. But then he pulled his mouth from mine, his lips all swollen, his eyes unfocused and heavy-lidded, and he started to move down my body. Slowly, kissing his way down my neck, my chest, he paused and looked up at me. "This okay?"

"Very fucking okay."

He smiled and kissed down further, planting kisses down to my navel and down further still and he brushed his nose to my aching cock before he looked up again. "This okay? Because we're covered in come and you smelling of my sex is so fucking hot."

"Please, Troy," I begged. I threaded my fingers through his hair. "Please."

He bit his lip. "You did say if I wanted to suck your dick, I only had to ask."

I couldn't help it, I laughed. Then he ran his flattened tongue up the length of me, and oh God. Then he took me into his mouth, and I let my head fall back onto the airbed and put my hands over my face, trying to rein in the pleasure, the emotion.

He pulled off. "Look at me when I suck your dick."

His words and his tone almost made me come. I did as he demanded, leaning up on my elbows, and when our gazes locked, he slowly opened his mouth and took me in again.

"Oh, fuck," I whispered. "Troy."

He smiled with satisfaction as he slid down my shaft, his eyes never leaving mine. He hummed around me before coming off and sucking on the head. "You taste so good," he murmured, before tonguing my slit.

"You're gonna make me come," I warned him. He smiled victoriously and took me in again, deeper this time, sucking and tonguing. I couldn't hold back my orgasm. I put my hand to his jaw, feeling his cheek hollow in when he sucked, and never broke eye contact. "I'm coming."

Still leaning on one elbow, my other hand cupping his face, I let my head fall back as I came. Troy never pulled off, he just sucked harder—sucked my orgasm right out of me—and drank everything I gave him.

I couldn't move. I couldn't even blink. My brain was scrambled, my body was boneless. Troy crawled up over me and chuckled as his face appeared above me. "You dead?"

"Yep." I grabbed his chin and brought his lips to mine, tasting myself on his tongue. When we broke for air, I said, "You're gonna need to give me a minute. My brain's short-circuited."

Troy laughed and settled his weight on me, pressing his rock-hard cock into my belly, and he groaned. I rolled us over. His grin was wicked. "Thought you were out of action."

"Not with you turned on and groaning like that," I said. "Now it's my turn."

I pulled his shirt up and kissed his chest, rubbing his nipple between my lips. He squirmed. "Don't you mean my turn?"

I sat between his legs and gripped his cock. It was a gorgeous dick, a good seven inches, thick and veiny with a bulb head. It made my mouth water. "Nope, believe me, I'll enjoy this more than you will." I licked him first, tasting his precome, before taking him in my mouth. I pulled on his balls, letting my fingers wander back a little. With my free hand, I pumped the base of his cock while I sucked on the head.

Troy's thumb swiped the corner of my mouth and when I looked up at him, he was staring at me with a look of lust and wonder in his eyes. "Cal, oh Cal."

I sucked harder and he groaned louder. My God, he was vocal in bed. Another thing I never knew about him. Another thing I loved about him...

His body jerked underneath me, and he made some guttural sound deep in his throat. "Gonna come," he grated out.

I sucked him harder and he moaned, long and loud. His

balls drew up and his cock swelled in my mouth before he came down my throat. I swallowed him down and licked him clean before kissing my way back up to his neck, where I promptly buried my face and collapsed on top of him.

Troy slid his arm around me and pulled the sleeping bag over us and kissed the side of my head. The storm sounded like it had eased a little, not that either of us were getting up to check. I was warm against him, and all I could smell was Troy and sex. I wasn't getting up for no one.

———————

I WOKE to circles being drawn on my back and scratchy stubble at my cheek. Troy's voice was rough and close. "Thought you said I was the one who napped after sex."

I stretched and snuggled right back into him. "It's not raining," I said, stating the obvious.

"And it's getting dark outside."

I sat up then. "Have we been in here all afternoon?"

Troy smiled at me. "Any regrets?"

I looked right into his eyes. "None. You?"

He shook his head slowly. "None. Only that I have to put clothes on and go take a piss. I've been busting for ages."

"You should have woke me."

Troy smiled shyly. "Not for anything in the world."

I resisted the urge to say something smartarse back to him but settled for a quick kiss instead. Then I leaned over and grabbed his bag of clothes and handed it to him. I grabbed a dry shirt from my bag and pulled it over my head, then some clean, dry shorts. Troy quickly pulled on some shoes and undid the zipper to get out. He made a run for the tree line, and seeing the fire was well and truly too wet to relight, I grabbed some food out of the Esky and put it inside the tent. When Troy got back, I'd put the camper torch in the corner and was setting up a makeshift picnic on the airbed. "What's this?" he asked with a smile.

"A dinner of chips, apples, rice crackers, and cheese." I held up a bottle of water. "And there's beers too."

He grinned and took a seat, helping himself to some crackers. "Oh," he said, reaching for his bag. He revealed a deck of cards. "And these."

We spent the night playing cards, snacking and laughing, only stopping to kiss every now and again. But mostly we did as we'd always done. It was as though nothing had changed between us, only gotten better.

He was still my best mate, only with benefits.

When we'd had enough of cards, Troy unzipped both sleeping bags to make them like blankets, I turned off the torch, and we climbed under the covers. Only this time, I didn't have to pretend that his arm around me was deliberate, because now it was. "You warm enough?" he asked.

I was on my side next to him, my head on his chest and his arm wrapped around my shoulder. "Perfect."

"Well, today turned out better than I'd thought it would."

I gave him a bit of a squeeze. "Turned out okay, huh?"

"I thought for sure you'd tell me no," he admitted quietly.

"But you took the chance anyway."

"I did." He kissed the top of my head. "I had to. I was going crazy."

I leaned up and kissed him softly. "Me too. And for what it's worth, I'm really glad you did."

"I've been sleeping like shit because I've been worried about what would happen, ya know? It's all I've been thinking about. But tonight I reckon I'll sleep just fine."

I laughed and settled my head on his chest like it was my pillow. "If you can't sleep, feel free to wake me up."

I could feel his chest vibrate with quiet laughter. "Your wish. My command."

MAYBE IT WAS the cooler night, maybe it was Troy's body heat, maybe it was the relief that we'd finally gotten together—I don't know what it was—but I slept like a baby. From what I could tell, Troy didn't stir either.

But my bladder woke with the sun, and after a quick dash to the tree line, I ran back and dove straight back into bed.

"Argh, you're cold," Troy mumbled, pushing me away.

I stuck my feet on his and snuggled right into him. He shivered and bitched, but he ran his hands up my back. "You right now?" he asked.

"Much better."

He laughed. "And just for that, you can cook breakfast."

"How is that different to any other day?"

He gave me a squeeze. "It's not." Then he sighed. "I guess we have to pack everything up and go home."

"Well yeah, we can't stay here forever."

"I know. It'd be nice though, huh?"

"Yeah."

"Did you wanna get in some fishing before we leave?"

"For sure."

His grin was back. "Then you better get cracking on breakfast."

I gave him a shove but got out of bed. I cooked us a breakfast on the gas grill while Troy packed up inside the tent. When he came out, and the way he looked at me, I knew this thing between us would look different under the light of a new day. I knew his tell signs, and I could see Troy was a bit embarrassed and nervous. He bit his lip and ran his hand through his hair. "We okay?"

"I'm okay. You okay?"

"Yeah."

"Then we're okay," I said with a shrug. "Can you pass the eggs?"

Troy's eyebrows knitted together for the briefest moment. "Sure."

I was trying to act like nothing was different between us, when the truth was, it *was* different. So pretending wasn't going to work. "Are you talking about what we did yesterday and last night?"

"Well, yeah. Aren't you?"

I cracked the eggs onto the hotplate then looked right at him. "What we did was kinda great."

His smile was instantaneous, but it slowly flitted away. "But?"

"But nothing," I replied. "I was making you a high-protein breakfast so we could go for round two. If you wanted to, that is."

He laughed, much more relaxed, and sat down beside me. He picked up a burger bun in each hand and held them open for me. I put bacon on each, then the eggs. "Sunnyside up for me, overcooked rubber for you," I said. Then I squirted BBQ sauce onto his, just how he liked it, then tomato sauce onto mine.

"Thanks." The smile he gave me was a shy one. His cheeks were a little pink. He held my egg and bacon roll out for me. "You know how I like my breakfast."

"I know how you like most things." I bit into my brekky and he watched as I swallowed it down. "And after yesterday, I learned some new things."

He laughed as he chewed, though his embarrassment coloured his cheeks. He wouldn't look at me, so I tapped his foot with mine, and he finally made eye contact.

"I'd like to learn some more things," I said to him. "If you want."

He swallowed down his mouthful and nodded slowly. "I'd like that." Then his lips twisted and his eyes flinched. "I have to say something though. It'll probably ruin everything, but I can't not say this."

My breakfast forgotten, I stared at him and waited. When he didn't speak, I prompted him. "You can tell me anything."

"I can't do casual. Not with you. It's all or nothing." He licked his lips. "I don't mean to be demanding or whatever, and I know it's early days, but I had to tell you that. I can't do the friends with benefits thing with you. So tell me now if you're okay with that."

"All or nothing, huh?"

He was looking at his half-eaten burger when he nodded.

"Are you asking me to be your boyfriend?"

His head shot up and his eyes were wide. I'd never seen him look so vulnerable. "I don't know what I'm asking. I just have to be honest with you, that's all. I can't do casual because it wouldn't be enough for me, especially when it comes to you."

I put my burger down and knelt in front of him. I cradled his jaw with both hands and took a moment to look over his face. "It wouldn't be enough for me either. I want more than that for us. So if that makes me your boyfriend, then I'm happy with that."

He smiled so beautifully. His eyes crinkled at the sides, and he chuckled nervously. I leaned in and kissed him. "Boyfriend. I like the sound of that."

He was happier then, and after Troy cleaned up from breakfast, we lay everything out in the sun to dry. We worked well as a team; we always had. We fished until the sun was directly above us, and when we got back to camp, we packed up the tent and loaded everything into the ute.

Troy was tying off the rod holder, and when he turned around, I pushed him up against his ute and kissed him. "I keep forgetting I can do that now," I said when we broke apart. "I was just looking at you and thinking how fucking hot you were when I remembered that I could kiss you when I want."

He wiped his thumb across his bottom lip. "You can kiss me like that any time you like."

I studied him for a second. That little line between his

eyebrows was a tell of his I knew well. "You're worried about going home, aren't you?"

He chuckled and looked to the ground. "Well, there's a downside I never expected. You knowing me better than anyone else means I can't get away with shit."

I laughed at that. "That's exactly right." I took his hand and waited for him to look at me. "There's no need to worry about anything. We're good, aren't we? Boyfriends, yes?"

He smiled. "Yeah. I'm just worried. Overthinking everything, as per usual."

I put my hand to his jaw and lifted his chin so he would look into my eyes. "We're good, Troy. I'll tell you every day if you need to hear it."

He gave me an embarrassed, half-smile, but he nodded. So I kissed him again, pulling his bottom lip between mine. "Come on, reality is waiting for us back home. And so is Meggs. She'll kill me in my sleep tonight if I'm not home soon."

"Your cat's a little bit psycho."

"She likes you. And anyway, she's my *Hawaii Five-0* buddy. She appreciates Steve McGarrett as much as I do."

Troy rolled his eyes, but he was back to smiling. "You ready then?"

"As I'll ever be."

———

WE UNPACKED the ute at his place and decided, given it was almost five in the afternoon, that we'd go to our respective homes. We both had shit to do before work in the morning, and given we were both tradies, we started early. I needed to get some groceries, do some laundry, that kind of thing.

But after I'd had dinner and a shower, I planted my arse on my couch and sent Troy a text. *Hey.*

Hey.

I'm regretting my decision to not stay longer at your place.

You can always come over.

I looked at my watch. It was seven-thirty. I knew if I went to his place, we wouldn't be sleeping any time soon. *Not tonight, but what are you doing tomorrow night?*

Cooking you dinner.

I grinned at my phone. *Sounds good.*

Hey, ever had phone sex?

No…

I was expecting a text message, but instead my phone rang in my hand. His name flashed up on the screen. "That was quick."

"Never one to let an opportunity pass." I could hear the smile in his voice. "You in bed yet?"

"No. It's seven-thirty."

"That's disappointing. Phone sex could have been fun."

"Does phone sex on the couch not count?"

"I want you to spread out, lube up your arse…"

I didn't hear how that sentence ended. I was too busy walking to my room. I threw the lube onto my bed and climbed on after it. "Okay. On the bed, have lube. What's next?"

He guided me through, talking me to orgasm, his voice like velvet in my ear. It was every imagined fantasy come to life. For years when I'd laid in bed and fantasised about being with him, it was his voice, whispering dirty things in my ear, that brought me undone.

The only thing missing was his warm body wrapped around mine.

"You still there?" he asked.

I was breathless. "Yeah."

"Don't fall asleep just yet," he said before the call clicked off in my ear.

That was strange, even for him. I shot him a text. *You okay?* I threw my phone onto the bedside table and went into the bathroom to clean myself up. I'd no sooner done that and pulled on a pair of old trackies and a T-shirt when there was a knock on my front door.

It was Troy. He was wearing tracksuit pants and a shirt like me, and he looked windswept and a little worried or nervous. I pulled him inside. "What's up?"

He put his hands to my face and kissed me. Urgent and hard, then soft and slow. He pressed his forehead to mine and kept his eyes closed. "I needed to be here."

I nodded. "Okay. I'm glad you are." I took his hand and led him to my bedroom. He toed out of his sneakers then, fully dressed, climbed into my bed. I quickly joined him, and pulling him against me, I reefed up the blankets and wrapped him up in my arms. He breathed in deep, and I could feel the tension leave his body.

His face was against my chest, his hair smelled washed, and his usual scent of Old Spice filled my senses. "Your bed smells of you and sex," he whispered.

I snorted. "Because you made me come."

He chuckled, then went quiet for a moment. "Thank you. For not freaking out when I just showed up."

I kissed the top of his head. "Wanna tell me wassup?"

His answer was so softly spoken I barely heard him. "I didn't want this weekend to end."

"I'm not going anywhere," I whispered. His hold on me tightened, and he was soon asleep.

In the morning, he was gone.

CHAPTER SIX

I UNDERSTOOD we both started work at six-thirty, so leaving early was a given. I knew that. I just thought he would have woken me or left a note or a message. But he didn't. And I couldn't deny I was disappointed.

For the first hour of work, my disappointment became hurt. I wondered what I'd done wrong. Or did he wake up and realise he'd made the biggest mistake of his life?

Then for the second hour of work, my disappointment and hurt became anger. I was pissed at him for just bailing on me like that. Him, of all people. I checked my phone a dozen times, but there was nothing…

Then in the third hour of work, it hit me. I was dealing with Troy. My Troy. A man I knew better than I knew myself, and it occurred to me, that him leaving this morning wasn't about me at all.

My boss clicked his fingers in my face. "You in there, son?" he asked. "You've been moping around all mornin', now you're standing there with a stupid grin on your face."

I laughed. "Yeah, I'm good. I'm real good. But I've gotta go. I'll make the hours up, I promise."

I didn't wait for an answer. I just ran to my truck and got

in. I checked my watch. It was ten to ten. I took off like a scalded cat, and five minutes later I pulled up in his driveway and waited.

For approximately four minutes. It was crazy how well I knew him.

Troy pulled into his drive, and the look on his face was a mix of happiness and reservation. Shit. This is what I didn't want. This is why crossing that threshold from friends to lovers was never a good idea. I didn't want him to look worried or sad or scared when he saw me. We needed to sort this out now.

He got out of his ute slowly. "Hey."

"Hey," I replied.

He checked his watch. "What are you doing here? I mean, aren't you supposed to be at work?"

"Aren't you?" I retorted. "I'm here because I know you."

"What?"

"Let me guess. You woke up this morning at my place and panicked, then as you had your morning coffee, you got to thinking 'What have I done?' and after your first hour at work you were sure you'd made a mistake, and by morning tea time, your mind was going a million miles an hour, thinking we'd fucked up our friendship."

He bit his lip and looked away. "Maybe."

I laughed. "Exactly. You did the same thing when we came out to our families. You did the same thing before your final exams."

He smiled and I knew I was right. He looked right at me. His eyes were bright with uncertainty and a flicker of fear. "Can we talk inside?"

I followed him inside to the kitchen, and he switched on the kettle. Then he turned and leaned his arse against the counter. He was fidgeting his hands until he shoved them into his pockets. When I thought he was going to say something, he let out a long breath instead.

"Troy," I started softly. I stood in front of him, as emotionally exposed as he was. "What are you thinking? Tell me. You've never not been able to talk to me."

"I know. And that's what I'm scared of," he said. He looked away, out the kitchen window, like looking at me was too hard.

"Scared of what?"

His gaze shot to mine. "Of losing what we have," he said. "Of risking it all. You've been my best friend forever, and I don't know what I'd do without you, and that scares me."

"Oh."

Before I could gather my thoughts, he added, "See? It's already changed us. We can't talk like we normally do."

"Do you not want us to take this further?"

His eyes widened, and he barked out a laugh. I'd never seen him so on edge before. "Don't you get it? That's what terrifies me. Not trying. Not seeing if this could be the best thing to ever happen to me. That's what scares me, Cal. You telling me it's not what you want. That's what scares the shit outta me."

I couldn't help but smile a little. I pulled his hand out of his pocket and threaded my fingers with his. "I'm telling you, it is what I want. Yes, things are going to change, and yes, it's all new. But I want it. I think you and I could be something special."

I slid my free hand along his jaw, and his lips parted a little. His eyes were liquid amber, and his chest was heaving. I leaned in slowly, almost touching his lips with mine but stopping an inch short. His pupils blew out, and I'm sure he stopped breathing. I ghosted my lips over his, barely touching at all. The heat of his body set my blood on fire.

Troy gasped, and that was all it took. I crashed my mouth to his and he moaned when he pulled me against him. I pushed him against his kitchen counter, our bodies touching from thighs to our mouths, our tongues tasting, our hands touching, holding.

When he pulled away to breathe, his lips were plump and wet, his eyes were dark. "Cal." My name was just a whisper. He'd never said my name like that before. Like he wanted me, like a prayer. With his eyes closed, with his forehead pressed to mine, he said, "So are we doing the real boyfriends thing? Now it's just not a weekend thing?"

"It was never just a weekend thing, Troy. Is that what you were worried about? That we'd come back to real life and I'd change my mind?"

His face twisted and he half shrugged. "I love you Cal, and it scares me because, now I've been with you, I know there'll never be anyone else for me. I've been in love with you since the eighth grade."

I leaned back a little, so I could put a finger to his chin and lift his face. "Look at me." I waited for him to. There was so much vulnerability in his eyes. My heart was in my throat, but if he was putting it all on the line, then I could too. "I've been in love with you since then too. I love you, Troy, and like I told you last night, I'm not going anywhere."

His smile was immediate, and it became a bubble of relief and laughter. He put his hand to my face, and his gaze took in my every feature like he couldn't believe I was this close. "What do we do now?"

"Well, considering we're both off work today, it'd be a shame to waste it," I said. "How about bed, then lunch, then more bed?"

He grinned. "It would be a shame to waste it, wouldn't it?"

I kissed him softly, and then my phone rang. I pulled it from my pocket, thinking it would be my boss, but it wasn't. I put it to my ear. "Yes Peta?" I answered with a smile.

"So? Give me details. What happened with Troy? You spent the weekend alone fishing, please tell me you got the catch of the century. Or do you still have your head up your arse?" Her words all ran together.

Troy laughed, clearly hearing every word. I shut him up by quickly pressing my lips to his. Though he was quick to answer for me, "Peta, I'm pretty sure *I* got the catch of the century."

There was a beat of silence as Peta clearly processed what she heard. Then a burst of laughter. "Oh my God, I knew it! Wait, why aren't you two at work? Oh. Nope, don't answer that. If you're both not at work, what the hell are you doing answering your phone. Jesus Cal. Are you in bed? Did you answer your phone while you're in bed together?"

Troy was trying not to laugh, and I snorted into the phone. "No, we're not in bed. Yet. I did just suggest it however."

Peta laughed, and Troy took my phone. "He'll call you back later tonight. Maybe." He disconnected the call and threw my phone onto the kitchen bench. "Now, if we're going to do the whole best friends-to-lovers thing, we'd better go about it properly, yeah?"

That made me smile. "I thought we crossed that line already."

"We frotted the line."

I burst out laughing. "Then we better cross it more thoroughly."

Troy chuckled, then with a deep breath, he took my hand. "If we do this, we can't go back."

"I know."

"No regrets?"

"No regrets."

His smile was breathtaking, half desire, half nervous. He took my hand and started to walk backwards, leading me down the hall to his room. Except he walked right into the wall. He turned around, like the wall surprised him, half laughing.

"You don't want to look where you're going?"

"I don't want to *not* see your face," he replied, then shook his head like he didn't mean to say that out loud. "I mean, I'm taking you to my bedroom... I don't want to miss anything..." His words trailed away unfinished.

Smiling, I stepped right in close and kissed him. "Believe me, you won't."

This time, I led him—facing the way I was walking—with my hand holding his behind me. I felt braver than I should have. I mean, I was nervous, but this felt right.

His room was as it always was. His bedcovers were dark grey, the curtains were still closed, the room was muted light and warm. My eyes were drawn back to his bed. It was kinda high and looked real soft. Even after all the years I'd known him, I'd never been in his bed. I don't think I'd even sat on it. A thrill ran through me at the thought of what was about to happen.

I turned to find him staring at me. His lips slightly parted, his eyes dark. "I'm nervous," he whispered.

I'd never known Troy to be nervous about anything. I took both his hands. "Why?"

"Because it's you. Because I've waited my whole damn life for this." He swallowed hard. "What if... what if you think I'm no good in bed? What if this is over in like thirty seconds, because there's a pretty good chance that'll happen."

I pulled him closer to me and kissed him with smiling lips. I didn't want him to freak out any more than he already had, so I said, "You're overthinking it. Don't be nervous. It's just me."

He still seemed unsure. His licked his lips nervously. "You're not nervous at all?"

I shook my head slowly. "Because it's you. And I know you'd never laugh at me or hurt me. Part of me was nervous, but nothing has ever felt more right than it does right now."

He stared at me and I could see the shift in his eyes. His

shoulders relaxed and he let out a deep breath. "You're right. Of course you're right."

I slid my hand along his jaw and bought my lips to within half an inch of his. "I'm always right," I whispered. He smiled, and I kissed him then, hard and deep, sliding my tongue into his mouth. He moaned and leaned into me in the most delicious way. Like he was at my mercy. I pulled my mouth away, leaving him heavy lidded and starry eyed. My voice was gruff when I asked, "How do you want to do this?"

"You, in me," he whispered. "I always fantasised that you would..." He didn't finish his sentence, but his cheeks flushed pink.

God, this shy Troy was new to me. "You've fantasised that I would what? Take you to bed and fuck you?"

His breath hitched. "Jesus, you're trying to kill me."

I put my fingers to his chin and made him look at me. "Only in the very best of ways. I never knew you were so shy in the bedroom."

"I'm not normally," he replied quickly. "But this is you."

I lifted the hem of his shirt up and pulled it over his head. His nipples pebbled and his breaths became rapid. I ran my hand over his chest watching the wake of goose bumps that rippled from my touch. "Fuck, Troy. You're so responsive."

He pulled my shirt over my head. "Cal, I swear, if you don't do something to me soon, I'm pretty sure I'll die."

I kissed the bare skin on his shoulder and trailed my mouth up to his ear. "Right. I'll tell you how this will happen. I'm going to lay you on that bed and I'm gonna fuck you until your body can't take any more. Then later on, you'll do me. How does that sound?"

His breath hitched and he nodded, quickly undoing his work pants. He ripped off his boots like they were on fire, then pulled his pants off, leaving only briefs. His cock was hard and pressed against his hip, snug in the material that confined him. Fuck, he was glorious. He was everything I'd imagined he would be. And he was mine for the taking.

No, not even that. He was mine. Just mine.

Emotions overwhelmed me at that realisation. I rested my forehead on his shoulder and trailed my nose up to the back of his neck. My voice was barely a whisper. "Lay on the bed, on your back."

He did as I asked, turning in time to watch me strip. I pulled off my boots and socks, lifted my shirt over my head, and popped the button on my work pants. He stared at my open fly and palmed his dick. A wet spot appeared on his briefs at the bulbous head. God, it made my mouth water. I licked my lips and had to tear my gaze from his groin to his face. "Lube? Condoms?"

He looked surprised at my question, like he was too distracted by the hair from my navel that trailed down to my briefs. His gaze shot to mine and he blinked. "Uh, bedside table."

I found what I was after in the top drawer and threw it onto the bed beside him. Then I knelt on his bed and crawled over to him. "I've waited a long time for this," I said, my voice was thick with desire. I positioned myself between his legs, sat back on my haunches, and ran my hands up his thighs. "I want to savour every detail."

Troy squirmed and palmed his dick again. "Cal, you're killing me here."

Keeping my gaze locked with his, I leaned down, and nudged the bulge in his briefs. His scent was intoxicating. I slowly pulled the elastic down and revealed his cock. "Oh fuck," I let out on a breath. His cock was thick and a vein ran from the base to tip. He was cut, his cockhead a plump purple. I couldn't help it. I had to taste it. I swiped my tongue delicately across the slit, and his thighs tightened.

"Cal. Stop teasing me, or this'll be over real quick."

I licked up his shaft. "Don't hold back. If you want to come, then come."

He groaned and fell back onto the mattress. He put his hands in his hair and rolled his hips. He was so close.

I picked up the lube and Troy sighed with relief. I smeared it over my fingers and rubbed his perineum and cupped his balls with my other hand. He hissed and bucked his hips, and he only calmed when I slipped a finger inside him. He groaned long and low when I added a second finger. "Cal," he murmured. "Oh God, Cal."

Without pulling my fingers out, I reached up with my other hand and grabbed the small foil packet at his side. I put it on his belly. "Can you open it?"

He tore at the packet and held it out for me. I shook my head. I pulled my fingers out of him and took off my underwear. I went back between his thighs and knelt with my cock pointing right at him. "Put it on me."

His eyes went dark and his chest heaved with ragged breaths. "Jesus, Cal." He sat up and, taking my cock in his hands, rolled the latex sheath down my length. His touch felt like fire: warm, delicious, and all-consuming. While he was still sitting up, I took his face in my hands and kissed him, hard.

I pushed him back down so I was on top of him. He spread his legs wide, bringing his knees up to our chests, offering himself to me. I kissed him deeper, tilting my head to kiss him harder. He broke the kiss to breathe and to beg. "Please."

His cock was leaking liberally on his belly. I gripped him, but he stopped me. "I want to come with you inside me," he whispered.

Oh fuck. Hearing those words from him… I positioned the head of my cock at his hole and leaned over him as I slowly slid inside him.

Troy's eyes widened and his breath fluttered as I breached

him. He felt so good, but it was more than physical. This was so much more. I was overcome with ecstasy and emotion. Every nerve in my body was singing, it felt so good—it was more than physical. I knew why. It was my heart telling me my soul had finally met its match.

And by the way Troy looked at me, I knew he felt it too.

I pushed all the way into him, slowly and deeply. I nudged his nose with mine and ghosted my lips over his. "This is... you are... everything," I whispered against his mouth.

He replied with his body; his arms hooked around my shoulders and he lifted his arse to meet me. I thrust into him harder, getting that perfect angle, making his eyes roll back in his head. I kissed him then, tasting his tongue, wanting him to feel all of me.

He moaned into my mouth and arched his back. His neck corded, his eyes wide, his mouth open, and he came in thick, hot spurts between us.

He was magnificent.

I thrust into him again and again as his orgasm washed through him, and I couldn't hold back any longer. Troy held my face as I came, staring into my eyes and watching every emotion I couldn't contain.

"Oh, Cal," he breathed. He nodded, and I had no clue what questions he'd asked in his own mind or what answers he saw on my face, but it was clearly a powerful one. His amber eyes glistened, and he nodded again before bringing my face into his neck and wrapping his arms tight around me.

Neither of us spoke for a while. It was a resonating silence, an appropriate void where I could only hear his heart and mine. He drew circles with his fingertips on my back, and I nuzzled into his neck and sighed. I pulled out of him and rolled us onto our sides, with him in my arms, and we dozed.

When I woke up, his face was just a few inches from mine

and he was staring at me. I brushed his hair from his fore-head, and I couldn't look away from his eyes. "Your eyes have flecks of gold and brown," I murmured.

He smiled. "I know."

"I've never seen them this close up."

He kissed me softly. "And your eyes are the colour of beef and Guinness pie."

I barked out a laugh. "You're hungry, aren't you?"

He grinned. "Starving."

"I'll make you something. Stay here, I'll go clean up a bit then bring you food."

Before I could detangle myself from him completely, he pulled me back. His face was just an inch from mine. "What we just did was perfect. I need you to know that. It was like you said, it was everything I thought it would be. And more. I'm in love with you, Cal. And I've never made love before, but that's what that was, yeah?"

I nodded. "Yeah, I'm pretty sure it was." I kissed him sweetly. "I've never experienced that with anyone else. That connection. I mean, for me there's never really been anyone else. There was only you. It was always you. Since I was four-teen years old and you told me you liked boys too. It's been you."

His smile was slow spreading, and his eyes glittered with light and happiness. "Me too."

He let me roll out of bed this time, and when I discarded the condom and pulled on some pants, he lay there and never took his eyes off me. "You right there? Ogling me like a piece of meat."

With the sheets around his waist, he was looking all sorts of perfect, and he grinned without shame. He put his hands behind his head. "Yep. You should probably get used to it. It might take me a while to stop. I've spent years wanting to touch you and shoving my hands in my pockets so I didn't."

He bit his lip. "And now I don't have to. Shove my hands in my pockets, that is."

I chuckled at him. "No you don't. You can shove them in mine."

He sighed contentedly and took a long minute to look me over some more. When his gaze finally met mine, he smirked. "How's my sandwich coming along?"

"Fuck you."

"You just did. Sandwich first, then round two, yes? Wasn't that the plan?"

I smiled at him. "That was the plan."

"So make it quick. Don't you think we've wasted enough time? Like ten years. We've got a bit of making up to do."

"I suppose I have to get used to your bossiness for real now, huh?"

He grinned hugely. "You've been putting up with it for years. I think you'll cope."

"I'm sure I will."

"Cal?"

"Yeah?"

"Sandwich."

I snorted out a laugh. "Yeah, yeah." I did make him a ham and tomato sandwich, grabbed some juice, some grapes, and a bag of chips, and brought the whole lot back on a tray. I was expecting some smartarse comment, but he was sound asleep. I had to wonder if he'd spent the whole night in my bed awake and scared. He was now lying on his stomach, his left leg bent at the knee, his arms under his pillow, and the sheet now revealed two perfect little divots above his backside. I'd never noticed them before.

I slid the tray on the bedside table, knelt on the bed, and crawled up his legs. I pressed kisses to the dimple above his left butt cheek, then the dimple on the right side, and intermittently up his spine. I kissed the back of his neck, and he replied with a moan. "Still hungry?" I murmured.

"Hmm," he answered sleepily.

"Food? Or nap?"

"Both."

I climbed off him and put the tray of food on the bed beside him. He rolled over and leaned against the headboard, and I gently climbed back onto the bed and sat beside him, my legs out in front, and put the tray on my lap. I handed him half the sandwich and he hummed appreciatively as he ate it. I ate the other half, then plucked some grapes and handed them to him as well. "It's a well proven fact grapes are effective in endurance. You know, for later."

He popped one in his mouth and crunched it. "Is that right? I thought you were going to compare them to testicles and see how I handled one in my mouth."

I laughed. "Just one? I had hopes for two."

He snatched up two grapes and sucked them into his mouth, one at a time, from the palm of his hand. Then he tongued them skilfully and made an indecent sound in the back of his throat. I stared at his mouth until his lips became a smirk. He bit the grapes, snapping me out of my filthy daydreams, and he laughed. "I had no idea you were so easy," he said.

I sipped my juice, hoping he wouldn't notice how my cheeks were heated. I swallowed my drink and remembered that I didn't have to hide anything from him anymore. I looked right at him and said, "Just for you."

Troy's eyes softened, and he slid his hand over mine. "Promise?"

"Promise what?"

"That's it's just me," he said, suddenly serious.

"Yes. It's just you. Well, you and Lieutenant Commander Steve McGarrett."

Troy laughed, but it was tight and his eyes flashed with uncertainty. I knew that look. He needed a strictly honest answer.

I met his gaze and took a deep breath. "Troy, you know me. I'm strictly a one man guy. I would never ruin this."

"Good," he said with a relieved sigh. Then he swallowed hard. "Because Cal, I haven't really even looked at another guy. Ever. I mean, there's been other guys." He cringed. "But none of them were you."

I leaned in and put my hand to his face before I kissed him. "Troy, you're it for me. Not just for the weekend, not just casual. I'm thinking it could probably be forever. So you'd better get used to it."

His shy smile pressed the dimple into his cheek. "Will you make me sandwiches when I'm hungry?"

"Always."

His voice dropped an octave. "Will you fuck me like you did before?"

"Whenever you need it."

He licked his lips and his pupils dilated. "Cal..."

"Yeah?"

"I'll sit through *Hawaii Five-0* with you," he said, completely serious. "And I'll take you fishing anytime you want. And I'm not great with words, but I'll try to tell you how great you are all the time. And we can fix up your house together. Well, you can, and I'll help or watch or something. And you do stuff for me, like making me sandwiches, and it makes me feel special that you think of me. I want to do things for you too. I want to be a better person because of you, for you." He shrugged. "Sorry, I just had to say that. If I don't say it now, I'm not sure I will."

That was a declaration of love from him if I'd ever heard one. I kissed him with smiling lips. "I love you too."

He laughed, embarrassed. "I do. Love you, that is. I always have."

"Me too."

He sat back, all happy-like, and sighed. "I guess we

should call our folks. My mum is gonna freak. You know, sometimes I think she loves you more than me."

I snorted out a laugh. "Later. We have a nap and more sex to have first."

"Oh yeah?"

"Yeah, and anyway, you shouldn't do unspeakable things with grapes in front of me like that."

He chuckled. "I'll keep that in mind."

I got off the bed and put the tray back on the bedside table. I collected another condom from the drawer while I was at it and threw it beside him. "Sex first?"

He smirked. "I thought we were gonna nap first."

I pulled my shorts down and crawled onto my side of the bed next to him and lay on my stomach. I might have raised my arse a little and moaned. Maybe. "Well, you can nap. I'll start without you."

He pounced on me, a knee either side of my hips, and his hands pinned my arms to the mattress above my head. "No starting without me. I've waited too damn long for this happen. I don't care if we never sleep again."

I rolled my hips for him. "At this rate, I don't think we will."

He kissed the back of my neck, then all the way down my spine. "Peta's right, you know," he said, softly kissing the top of my arse. "You're the perfect catch."

"No catch and release program here."

"Nope. Hook, line, and sinker. You're a keeper."

There was a beat of silence before we both cracked up laughing. I rolled over onto my back, and he settled on top of me between my legs. We were both turned on, but we were both grinning as well.

"No more bad fishing puns," I pleaded.

"Deal." He kissed me with smiling lips. "When does *Hawaii Five-0* start?"

"Seven o'clock. Why?"

He looked at his watch. "Gives us eight and a half hours."

"What for?" I gave him daring look. "You gonna fit the last ten year's worth of sexual frustration in in eight hours?"

He hitched my thigh up, making me grunt, and he kissed me. "I'm sure as hell gonna try."

"Oh, and don't think I haven't forgotten about you making me a three course dinner this weekend."

He kissed down my jaw. "No rush for that, right?" He gently bit my earlobe. "I mean, sometime between now and forever's okay, yeah?"

I took his face in his my hands and looked right into his eyes. "Forever sounds pretty good."

He crushed his mouth to mine, kissing me like he owned me. And he was right about making up ten years in eight hours.

He was right about forever too.

~ THE END

ABOUT N.R. WALKER

N.R. Walker is an Australian author, who loves her genre of gay romance. She loves writing and spends far too much time doing it, but wouldn't have it any other way.

She is many things; a mother, a wife, a sister, a writer. She has pretty, pretty boys who live in her head, who don't let her sleep at night unless she gives them life with words.

She likes it when they do dirty, dirty things...but likes it even more when they fall in love.

She used to think having people in her head talking to her was weird, until one day she happened across other writers who told her it was normal.

She's been writing ever since...

ALSO BY N.R. WALKER

Spencer Cohen Book Two

Spencer Cohen Book Three

Yanni's Story

On Davis Row

Free Reads:

Sixty Five Hours

Learning to Feel

His Grandfather's Watch (And The Story of Billy and Hale)

The Twelfth of Never (Blind Faith 3.5)

Twelve Days of Christmas (Sixty Five Hours Christmas)

Best of Both Worlds

Translated Titles:

Fiducia Cieca (Italian translation of Blind Faith)

Attraverso Questi Occhi (Italian translation of Through These Eyes)

Preso alla Sprovvista (Italian translation of Blindside)

Il giorno del Mai (Italian translation of Blind Faith 3.5)

Cuore di Terra Rossa (Italian translation of Red Dirt Heart)

Cuore di Terra Rossa 2 (Italian translation of Red Dirt Heart 2)

Cuore di Terra Rossa 3 (Italian translation of Red Dirt Heart 3)

Cuore di Terra Rossa 4 (Italian translation of Red Dirt Heart 4)

Intervento di Retrofit (Italian translation of Elements of Retrofit)

Confiance Aveugle (French translation of Blind Faith)

CPSIA information can be obtained
at www.ICGtesting.com
Printed in the USA
LVHW032113060420
652381LV00003B/381

9 781925 886221